D0955612

If the shoe fits

If the shoe fits

Krista Bell • Craig Smith

Charlesbridge

For girls and boys everywhere
who love to dance—K. B.

2008 First U.S. edition
Text copyright © 2008 by Krista Bell
Illustrations copyright © 2008 by Craig Smith

Published by Charlesbridge
85 Main Street
Watertown, MA 02472
(617) 926-0329
www.charlesbridge.com

First published in Australia in 2006 by Hachette Livre Australia Pty Ltd. This edition is published by arrangement with Hachette Livre Australia Pty Ltd.

Library of Congress Cataloging-in-Publication Data
Bell, Krista.
    If the shoe fits / Krista Bell ; illustrated by Craig Smith.
        p. cm.
    First published: Australia : Hachette Livre Australia Pty Ltd., 2006.
    Summary: Cassie wants to be a dancer when she grows up but is afraid to dance in front of anyone outside her family, until the day of her first jazz performance arrives and her mother and a new friend help her to gain confidence.
    ISBN 978-1-58089-338-1 (reinforced for library use)
    ISBN 978-1-58089-339-8 (softcover)
[1. Self-confidence—Fiction. 2. Jazz dance—Fiction. 3. Dance recitals—Fiction. 4. Dance—Fiction. 5. Friendship—Fiction.] I. Smith, Craig, 1955- ill. II. Title.
PZ7.B38915If 2008
[E]—dc22   2007027022

Printed in the United States of America
(hc) 10 9 8 7 6 5 4 3 2 1
(sc) 10 9 8 7 6 5 4 3 2 1

Illustrations done with a 2B graphite clutch pencil on tracing paper
Display type and text type set in Goudy and ITC Legacy Serif
Printed and bound by Lake Book Manufacturing, Inc.
Production supervision by Brian G. Walker
Designed by Paulene Meyer and Martha MacLeod Sikkema

chapter one

Cassie loved to dance.

At school one morning her teacher
asked the class what they wanted to be
when they grew up. When it was her
turn, Cassie was nervous.

"I want to be a dancer on television," stuttered Cassie. Her cheeks felt hot. "And I want to dance in a troupe at pop concerts." Her hands felt sweaty. "With famous singers like Stella." She felt funny. She had to sit down.

Cassie closed her eyes. She thought about how much she wanted to be a dancer when she grew up.

Cassie went to dance classes three times a week. On Mondays she had ballet class—ballet was graceful. Mondays were okay. On Thursdays she had tap class—tap was noisy. Thursdays were better.

On Saturday mornings she went to

jazz class—jazz was funky, totally cool.
Saturday was the best.

Except for one thing. There was a
problem. Well, there was more than
one problem.

chapter two

The first problem was that Cassie got really nervous if people were watching her dance.

Another problem was that she hadn't made a real friend in the class.

5

She knew she was silly for not wanting to dance in front of other people. At home with her family, she was fine. But going to dance classes was totally different. She felt shy, even in front of the other kids.

Why couldn't she be confident like Jake? He was such a show-off. Cassie didn't know him very well—he didn't talk much.

While Cassie hid in the back line, Jake would be up in front near their teacher, Miss Kaye. He was *so* confident.

But the real problem was that if she didn't like people watching her dance, how could Cassie be a dancer when she grew up? How would she dance on television? Or perform in a troupe at a pop concert?

And how would Cassie dance in front of all the parents at the end-of-term Open Day next Saturday?

Her own parents would be there—that was okay. But an audience—how would she dance in front of an audience?

Cassie felt sick just thinking about it.

Hey, that was it! She'd be "sick" next Saturday! Lots of kids had coughs and colds at the moment. Perfect. She would just say she was sick, cough a bit, and stay in bed. Problem solved. Or was it?

chapter three

When Cassie woke up on Saturday morning, her mother knew she wasn't sick. Moms always know that stuff—that's their job. So pretending to be sick was never going to work.

Cassie knew she had to dream up something else—but what? It was only one hour until dance class. She had to think of a good excuse—quickly.

There was no way Cassie was going to dance in front of all the other kids' parents and grandparents. No way.

"Mom, I can't go to jazz class today," Cassie said at breakfast. "My jazz shoes don't fit me anymore—they're too tight."

Cassie crossed her fingers behind her back. Her shoes were tight, but not that tight. She just couldn't dance in front of an audience.

"And we don't have time to go to the mall to buy a new pair. I'll just have to miss jazz class this week."

This was sure to work, wasn't it?

chapter **four**

"Don't worry, Cassie," her mother said as she put breakfast on the table. "New shoes are no problem."

Cassie frowned. What was her mother talking about?

"Don't you remember Miss Kaye's cupboard of secondhand shoes?" her mother asked. Cassie's heart sank. Of course. "I always bought your sisters'

15

dance shoes there. We'll go a bit earlier—we're sure to find you a pair before class."

Great—her mother had solved the problem. Now Cassie would have to dance at Open Day. She'd run out of excuses—except the real one. And she wasn't going to tell anyone about being afraid of an audience, not even her mother.

"The secondhand shoes are half the price of new ones," her mother added. "I'm looking forward to watching you perform. So are Dad and your sisters—we'll all be there."

"Great," Cassie said. "Great."

All she could think about was how, shoes or no shoes, she wouldn't be able to dance one step. She'd make a fool of herself.

If only she were like Jake. He was so confident. So out there. And even though he was a show-off, Cassie wished she could be a little bit like him. Was that so silly?

chapter five

The dance school studio was buzzing.
Parents and grandparents sat in rows,
waiting for the Open Day class to begin.

Cassie and her mother were hunting through the cupboard of secondhand shoes. So far they hadn't found the right size.

"They should be called second-foot shoes, don't you think?" laughed Cassie's mother. "They're not gloves, are they? So they shouldn't be called secondhand. Get it?"

Cassie's mother often made bad jokes to cheer Cassie up—but this time it wasn't working.

"Look! Here's a pair that belonged to Miranda Farren," said her mother excitedly. She had read the name on the bottom of the jazz shoes.

"Fancy these shoes still being here. Miranda Farren is the most famous dancer Miss Kaye ever taught. You know—the girl on television with the curly red hair. She dances in the troupe that backs that pop star. What's her name? Estella?"

Cassie just stared at her mother. Was this another of her jokes? No. She seemed serious.

"*Stella?*" Cassie asked. "Miss Kaye taught Stella's lead dancer? Really? That's so cool."

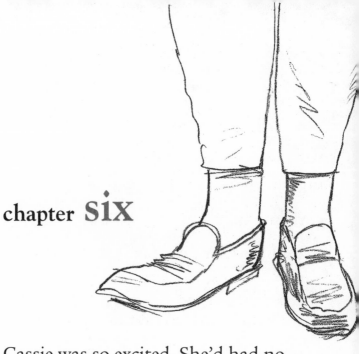

chapter six

Cassie was so excited. She'd had no idea Miss Kaye had taught such a famous dancer. Cassie tried on the secondhand jazz shoes that had belonged to Miranda Farren.
The shoes fit Cassie perfectly.

"How lucky are you?" asked Cassie's mother. "You know what they say: 'If the shoe fits, wear it!' Miranda Farren was always a beautiful dancer—even when she was young. From what I've seen of your dancing at home, you're just as good. Maybe better—especially in Miranda Farren's shoes, eh?"

Cassie didn't know why, but just wearing Miranda Farren's old jazz shoes made her feel special—and a bit more confident.

Maybe, just maybe, she *would* be able to dance in front of the audience. Miranda Farren was Cassie's idol—and she danced in front of thousands of people all the time. Could Cassie be like her? She hoped so.

Maybe she should dance next to Jake—that might help her be even more confident. Cassie took a big breath and walked to the front line of her class.

Jake wasn't there. The class was about to start. Looking at the audience, Cassie felt her cheeks go red. Where was Jake?

Cassie's hands began to sweat. Even wearing Miranda Farren's shoes, she wasn't sure that she could do this without Jake next to her. Cassie wiped her hands on her skirt.

Water. She needed a drink of water, but she'd left her water bottle in the locker room. She'd have to be quick —the class was about to start.

30

As she ran to the locker room, Cassie wondered why Jake wasn't in class. Was he sick? She hoped not. Maybe he was just late. Yes, he'd be there soon—he had to be.

Without Jake dancing next to her, Cassie might be in real trouble.

chapter seven

"Why are you sitting here?" Cassie asked Jake. She had almost fallen over him. "Our class is starting in a minute. Are you sick?"

But Jake just sat where he was on the locker-room floor. His shoulders were slumped, and his eyes seemed a bit red.

"Think I'll stay here," he mumbled.
"I don't want to dance."

"Don't be silly," laughed Cassie.
"You're our best dancer. We need you
in the front line—*I* need you."

What was wrong with Jake? This
was so unlike him. He was always so
confident. And Cassie was telling the
truth—she *did* need him.

"What's your problem?" asked
Cassie. "Can I help? Please, Jake. We've
got to hurry!"

But Jake just sat there looking at the floor.

"I think he wants me to be like him," he whispered. "I can't be. I can't dance today."

Cassie moved closer to Jake. This didn't make sense. Where was Jake the show-off when she needed him? Had he been crying?

"Who?" Cassie asked. "Who wants you to be like him?"

"My father," said Jake. "He's never ever seen me in class before. I can't dance with him here."

chapter eight

Cassie forgot all about her fear of
dancing in front of an audience. Jake's
problem seemed much worse. Cassie
didn't know how to help. She waited
for Jake to speak.

"My dad was a really good dancer," said Jake, "until he broke his leg in an accident. It happened before I was born. I love dancing, but I'm not him—I'm just me." He shrugged his shoulders and rubbed his eyes.

"Jake, you're a great dancer," said Cassie. "Don't worry about your dad. Show him how good you are.
You're the best.
He'll see that.
Trust me."

Jake smiled weakly and let Cassie
pull him up off the floor.

"Anyway, how come you need me
in class?" Jake asked Cassie. "You're an
excellent dancer—and why do you
always hide in the back? You belong in
the front line. You frightened or
something?"

Now it was Cassie's turn to shrug. She was pleased Jake thought she was a good dancer.

"I've never told anyone—I don't like dancing in front of people. Having an audience frightens me." There—she'd said it. It wasn't so bad. Jake hadn't laughed at her. That was a plus.

"An audience is just a bunch of people who wish they could dance like you," said Jake.

Cassie had never thought of it that way. Jake put on his jazz shoes without saying anything more. Did this mean he *would* dance?

How good would it be if he danced
next to her? And hey, she was wearing
Miranda Farren's shoes, wasn't she?

"Okay, tell you what." Cassie took
an enormous breath. "You dance next
to me in class, and I'll stay with you
when you see your dad
later. We'll do it
together.
Deal?"

"You bet. It'll be so cool having you in the front line," said Jake. "You really are a great dancer." He grabbed his water bottle out of his backpack. "And thanks, Cassie." He seemed shy for once.

"No worries," said Cassie. "You ready? Miss Kaye will wonder what's happened to us."

"Let's do it!" agreed Jake. "Race you!" As he disappeared out the locker-room door, Cassie ran after him laughing.

If her legs didn't start to shake, she and Jake could do this—together.

chapter nine

Miss Kaye was talking to the visitors as
Jake and Cassie joined the front line.
Holding her breath, Cassie looked

around the room. She could see her parents and sisters, but she didn't know Jake's parents.

Hang on—who was that woman with the long red curly hair sitting at the end of the front row? It couldn't be, could it?

"Ladies and gentlemen, boys and girls," said Miss Kaye. "I'd like to introduce our very special guest, Miranda Farren. Some of you already know that Miss Miranda is the patron of our dance school. And I'm thrilled that she's agreed to teach our show troupe next term."

Everybody clapped excitedly.
Cassie looked down at her feet. Wow!
She was wearing Miranda Farren's jazz
shoes—and Miranda Farren was here in
the dance studio! Next term she'd be
teaching the troupe.

How cool was that?

Cassie and Jake smiled at each other. Cassie hoped they'd both get chosen for the troupe. She had dreamed about dancing *like* Miranda Farren. Now she might get to dance *with* her as their teacher.

The music started for their first dance. Cassie knew that she and Jake both had something to prove. Jake had to show his father that he was a good dancer in his own right. Cassie had to relax and be confident dancing in front of an audience.

Impossible tasks?

Maybe, maybe not.

chapter ten

"Great to see you in the front line, Cassie," said Miss Kaye. "I knew it— you two were brilliant dancing together."

The class had been a success, and the visitors were having morning tea. Miss Kaye had taken Cassie and Jake aside.

"I was worried." Miss Kaye looked concerned. "I thought my two best dancers had run away! Is there a problem? Can I help?"

"No, we're fine, Miss Kaye," said
Cassie. "Sorry—we had to sort out some
stuff. But we're okay now, aren't we?"
She looked at Jake, who nodded but
still seemed unsure. He hadn't talked
to his father yet.

"Before you run off again," said
Miss Kaye, "I'd like you both to meet
Miss Miranda. I'm sure you've seen
her on television with Stella."

And before either of them could
say anything, Miss Kaye led them
toward Cassie's idol.

Cassie's chest heaved. She was
going to meet Miranda Farren. Her
face felt hot again. What would they
talk about? Quick—think! Okay.
Big breath.

"Hello, Miss Miranda," said Cassie excitedly. "I'm wearing your old jazz shoes. They're great to dance in. I just got them this morning—from the secondhand cupboard. They're really comfy." Cassie needed to take a breath.

Miss Miranda shook Cassie's hand. Then she shook Jake's.

"Is that your excuse? And what's yours, young man?" Miss Miranda joked. "You're both such talented dancers. I was never that good when I was your age. You're naturals. When Miss Kaye and I have finished with you, you'll be stars. Trust me. I'm really looking forward to teaching you both next term."

"We're in the troupe?" asked Cassie. She must be dreaming.

"You sure are," said Miss Miranda. "I'm not supposed to tell you this." She winked at Miss Kaye. "You were Miss Kaye's first choices. Congratulations."

"Thanks," Cassie and Jake said together. "This is so cool."

It was then that Cassie saw two sets of parents standing just behind Miss Miranda. All four were smiling proudly.

"Congratulations, Jake," said his father. "I had no idea you were such a great dancer. Blew me away! And getting into the troupe—well done."

Cassie smiled at Jake. All that worry for nothing—his father seemed so pleased.

"And for a girl who didn't even want to be here today, Cassie," said her mother, "you were wonderful. Those shoes certainly did the job! You and Jake danced so well together. And making it into the troupe is fantastic. You're a good team. Congratulations."

Cassie thought about this. She and Jake were better than a good team—they were a great team. And even better than that, they were friends. Real friends.